Milo's
trip to the Museum with grandpa

Created by Craig Ploetz
and Rich Koslowski

Milo Productions, Publishers
Milwaukee, Wisconsin

Milo's Trip to the Museum with Grandpa

Copyright © 1992 by Craig T. Ploetz and Richard K. Koslowski, Milo Productions.

Printed in the United States of America. All rights reserved.

Bound by Midwest Editions, Inc.

Printed by Litho Specialties, Inc.

Creative assistance by Sandra Koslowski.

Edited by SpectraCom, Inc. and Suzette Nelson.

Color separations and page assembly by National Graphics, Inc.

ISBN# 1-882172-01-9

Library of Congress Catalog Card Number 93-91466

This book is dedicated to both
the young and old who find the time
to share their adventures together.

Do you wonder about life in an earlier time,
before there were T.V.'s and telephone lines?
Have you ever seen mummies buried in stone,
insects and cavemen and dinosaur bones?

I know a place where these things can be found.
They're kept in a building made of marble, downtown.
One day my Grandpa and I went to see them,
these things in the building
they call the museum.

COUNTY MUSEUM

A man with a big smile opened the door, and asked us inside to roam and explore.

"Thank you," said Grandpa, "that's just what we'll do. We'll see some things old, and learn some things new."

Taking my hand and saying just that
Grandpa started our trip with a tip of his hat.
We walked to a room at the end of the hall
that looked like a forest with no ceiling or walls.

SOLAR SYSTEM

EGYPT

WELCOME TO THE
MUSEUM

DINOSAURS

INDIAN VILL

Once inside the trees
seemed to sway bringing
to life the things on display.
Birds and insects flew through the air as Indian children put braids in their hair.

EXIT

Wild rice was being carried
in deerskin sacks
by Indian mothers with
babes on their backs.

9

"What's going on here?" asked Grandpa, with a smile on his face.
"These things should not move, they should stay in one place."
But move they did, as a river appeared
carrying more Indians with fish they had speared.

"Come with us!"
they chanted.
"There's much
to be seen!"
So we
hopped
in canoes
and we
paddled
downstream.

As the boats moved along the water made swirls,
and the stories were told of a young Indian world.

They were tales of a people from a long time ago,
when brave Indian men hunted great buffalo.

They hunted and fished and worked the land,
and what the land could not give them, they made by hand.

They danced and sang of their brave way of life,
to the spirits of the animals on the ground and in flight.

Grandpa and I sang with them
as we paddled along,
but before we could thank them
our new friends had gone.

They smiled and waved as they said good-bye,
leaving many lessons for Grandpa and I.
They were lessons in life and respect for the land,
the love for family and the pride within man.

As our boat floated on we came upon four large trees that did not move in the blowing breeze.

They grew
up high into
the vines
and leaves,
so high,
their tops
we could
not see.

As our boat came closer,
we could hear munching sounds,
but who was munching
could not be found.
The river grew deeper
and darker downstream,
as we wound our way past
the four large trees.

Suddenly a
giant head
appeared!
It was long
and round.
It grabbed
Grandpa's hat
and gulped
it down!

20

"Dinosaurs!" Grandpa shouted.
"Those four trees are not part of the forest.
Those trees are the legs of a *Brontosaurus*!"

Grandpa was right.
It was a dinosaur,
that lived many,
many years before.
Before Grandpa
was born, before
the Indians too.
It lived in a time
when the earth
was new.

Grandpa was
surprised
at losing his hat.
"It eats only plants,
it should not have eaten that."

21

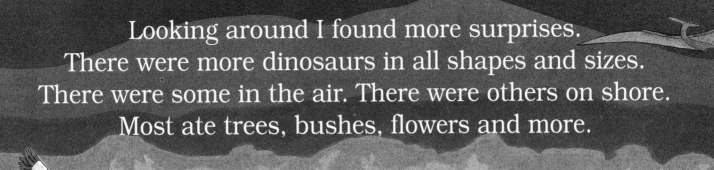

Looking around I found more surprises.
There were more dinosaurs in all shapes and sizes.
There were some in the air. There were others on shore.
Most ate trees, bushes, flowers and more.

Some had spikes. All had scales.
Some had horns, and all had tails.
One was no bigger than the size of a cat.
Another was the size of a whale.
One had giant plates on his back
that looked like they could have been sails.

All at once they stopped their chewing.
They could tell something bad in the forest was brewing.
Something they feared was coming our way,
its claws sinking deep into red forest clay.

We heard its roar and snapping teeth
as it pushed its way through nearby trees.
"What could it be?" Grandpa and I wondered.
"What could make dinosaurs hide, and roar like thunder?"

Closer and closer it came,
until it reached the edge of the forest.
It couldn't be...

but it was...

27

a TYRANNOSAURUS!

"*Tyrannosaurus rex,*" Grandpa said.
"The 'rex' part of its name means king.
This one's no plant eater,
he's a big meat-eating thing."

29

He looked very
hungry as he snapped
his teeth, and smacked his
lips at Grandpa and me.

30

We tried scaring away the hungry dinosaur
by jumping up and down and waving our oars.
But our boat tipped and started to lean
before throwing us both into the bubbling stream.

Grandpa told me to ride on his back
as the *Tyrannosaurus* moved in to attack.
Grandpa seemed fearless, as I held him tight.
He said, "If this one's looking for trouble
I'm up for the fight!"

He shook his fist
and called it names like
"lizard neck", "scale face",
and "salted peanut brain".

While this was going on,
something was tickling my feet.
Something was bubbling up
from way down deep.

Suddenly...

...**bursting** up through the water,
who did we see, but the first dinosaur with legs like trees.

It was the *Brontosaurus* that ate Grandpa's hat!
He had swung his tail 'round
and knocked the *Tyrannosaurus* flat!

We were safe on the back
of our new found friend,
but our trip to the museum
was close to an end.

The wind died down,
the trees stopped blowing,
the river dried up...

...and the walls were showing.
The moon disappeared
as night
turned
to day
and our
dinosaur friend
turned to bones
on display.

34

Everything was silent, then a voice from below
said we'd have to leave now, because the museum was closed.

It was the man with the smile
we had met at the door.
"Come back soon," said the man,
"there's much more to explore."

"So many things to see and places to travel,
worlds to visit and mysteries to unravel."

So, if you like wondrous things
I know where you can see them!
Make sure your next trip
is a trip to the museum!

Milo's Dinosaur Fun Facts

The *Tyrannosaurus* (tie - RAN - oh - SAW - rus), may be the most popular, and certainly is the largest carnivore found to date. A carnivore is a creature that eats meat. The giant jaws of the *Tyrannosaurus* enabled it to eat 200 pounds of meat in a single mouthful.
That's over 700 cheeseburgers in one bite!

One tooth from his great jaws could measure **7 inches** in length.

The fastest dinosaur known to date may have been the *Gallimimus* (GAL - ih - MIME - us), whose sleek legs could move it up to **35 miles per hour**.

Now you be an explorer.
Find the hidden objects on the listed pages.

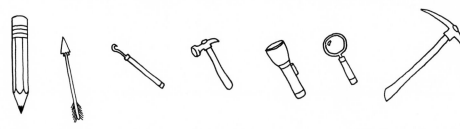

pencil	arrow	handpick	hammer	flashlight	magnifying glass	pickaxe
pg.6	pg.10	pg.12	pg.17	pg.19	pg.28	pg.34

Some of the creatures that lived among the dinosaurs look much like creatures that live with us today. Do you recognize some of these? All of them appear in the story except one. Which creature does not appear?   *Answer:*   *The possum does not appear.*

  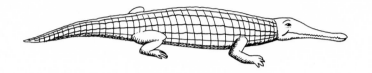  

One of the smallest known dinosaurs was the *Compsognathus* (komp - so - NAY - thus), which were about the size of a chicken.

The plant eating *Apatosaurus* (ah - PAT - oh - SAW - rus), more commonly known as the *Brontosaurus*, was one of the tallest dinosaurs that ever lived, standing close to 40 feet.

The tallest dinosaur known to date was the *Ultrasaurus* (ULL - tra - SAW - rus), measuring over 100 feet in length and standing **over 50 feet tall**. That means you could feed him from the roof of a five story building.

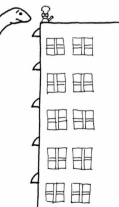